When Langston Dances

When
Langston

Dances

WRITTEN BY
KAIJA LANGLEY

ILLUSTRATED BY
KEITH MALLETT

A DENENE MILLNER BOOK
SIMON & SCHUSTER BOOKS FOR YOUNG READERS
NEW YORK   LONDON   TORONTO   SYDNEY   NEW DELHI

SIMON & SCHUSTER BOOKS FOR YOUNG READERS
An imprint of Simon & Schuster Children's Publishing Division
1230 Avenue of the Americas, New York, New York 10020
Text © 2021 by Kaija Langley
Illustrations © 2021 by Keith Mallett
Book design by Laurent Linn © 2021 by Simon & Schuster, Inc.
SIMON & SCHUSTER BOOKS FOR YOUNG READERS and related marks are trademarks of Simon & Schuster, Inc.
For information about special discounts for bulk purchases,
please contact Simon & Schuster Special Sales at 1-866-506-1949 or business@simonandschuster.com.
The Simon & Schuster Speakers Bureau can bring authors to your live event. For more information or to book an event,
contact the Simon & Schuster Speakers Bureau at 1-866-248-3049 or visit our website at www.simonspeakers.com.
The text for this book was set in Cantoria MT Std.
The illustrations for this book were rendered digitally.
Manufactured in China
0621 SCP
First Edition
2 4 6 8 10 9 7 5 3 1
Library of Congress Cataloging-in-Publication Data
Names: Langley, Kaija, author. | Mallett, Keith, illustrator.
Title: When Langston dances / Kaija Langley ; illustrated by Keith Mallett.
Description: First edition. | New York : Denene Millner Books, [2021] | Audience: Ages 4-8. | Audience: Grades K-1. |
Summary: Inspired by watching a performance of the Alvin Ailey Dance Company,
a young black boy longs to dance and enrolls in ballet school.
Identifiers: LCCN 2020020700 (print) | LCCN 2020020701 (eBook) |
ISBN 9781534485198 (hardcover) | ISBN 9781534485204 (eBook)
Subjects: CYAC: Ballet dancing—Fiction. | Sex role—Fiction. | African Americans—Fiction.
Classification: LCC PZ7.1.L34412 Wh 2021 (print) | LCC PZ7.1.L34412 (eBook) | DDC [E]—dc23
LC record available at https://lccn.loc.gov/2020020700
LC ebook record available at https://lccn.loc.gov/2020020701

For Langston, my Beloved, and dance lovers everywhere
—K. L.

To those who believe their dreams can come true
—K. M.

Langston liked basketball, but he *adored* ballet.

He fell in love the first time his mother took him to see the Alvin Ailey Dance Company. So many bodies soaring across the stage. Spinning, leaping, twirling dancers everywhere.

"Do you think I can dance like that?"
Langston asked his mother.
  "You can do whatever you set your mind
to doing," his mother said.

From that day forward, Langston practiced in front of his bedroom mirror. Finally, one Saturday morning he felt ready for his first day of school.

"Today is the day I dance," he told his mother as he double tied his sneakers.

"And you can dance to your heart's content," his mother said.

On the way to his new school, Langston told
everyone he met, "Watch me dance!"

He dipped for the mail carrier putting letters
in the box . . .

and kicked for the police officer helping them
cross the street . . .

and spun for the barber sweeping his sidewalk.

Langston waited for his applause. Instead, a kid passing by said, "Boys don't dance like that."

Langston huddled closer to his mother, but he replied, "They do too. I've seen them!"

When he arrived at Ms. Marie's Dance Studio, Langston felt nervous. Would the other students like the way he moved? Was he dressed properly in his basketball shorts and sneakers?

A gentle push from his mother, and Langston set off to find his class.

The first room was a class of students learning how to tap.

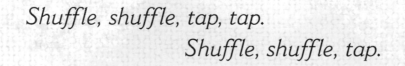

Shuffle, shuffle, tap, tap.
　　　　　Shuffle, shuffle, tap.

Langston wandered to the next class. He felt the "boom" from the music beneath his feet as students practiced hip-hop dance.

Another class of students clapped their hands and stomped their feet, keeping rhythm with a man beating a drum. They were learning African dance.

In the last classroom, the music was so quiet Langston could barely hear it. He watched excitedly as little girls stood in a line along the barre in front of a mirror and practiced the ballet positions as the dance teacher called them out.

"First position," she called.
When the girls moved their feet into the
shape of a V, Langston held on to the door
frame and followed their lead.

"Second position," the teacher announced next.
When the class slid one foot away, so did Langston.

Finally, Langston kicked off his sneakers and darted into the class to take his place at the barre. He closed his eyes and remembered the Alvin Ailey dancers.

The teacher clapped her hands to bring the class to attention. Langston opened his eyes and realized he stood alone in front of the mirror.

"Welcome to ballet. I am Ms. Marie," said the teacher. "I've been expecting you, Langston."

Langston took a bow.
"In this class we wear shoes." Ms. Marie
floated gracefully toward a closet.

She rummaged through a box and mumbled,
"*No. No. No,*" before exclaiming, "*Yes!*"

She handed Langston a pair of black ballet slippers.
They were different from the other students' slippers, but
he tried them on with delight. They fit him perfectly!

Overjoyed, Langston took off running
and leaping across the room.

He spun and jumped, dipped and
kicked. The girls gasped in wonder.

Ms. Marie nodded her approval. Then she clapped her hands again. "This is serious business. You must work very hard to be a ballet dancer. You'll have to earn those shoes, you know."

"I will," Langston said, standing taller than before.

The class lined up again along the mirror, and Langston took his place. He promised to work hard in every class. And Langston danced . . .

and danced . . .

and danced.